THIS BLOOMSBURY BOOK

BELONGS TO

....

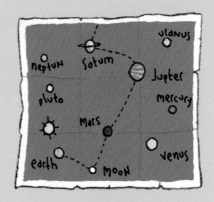

For my good friend Darran - RC

First published in Great Britain in 2001 by Bloomsbury Publishing Plc
38 Soho Square, London, W1D 3HB
This paperback edition first published in 2002

Text copyright © Frances Thomas 2001
Illustrations copyright © Ross Collins 2001
The moral right of the author and illustrator has been asserted

A CIP catalogue record of this book is available from the British Library
ISBN 0 7475 5569 9

Designed by Malena Wilson-Max
Printed in Hong Kong by South China Printing Co.

1 3 5 7 9 10 8 6 4 2

Maybe One Day

Frances Thomas and Ross Collins

BLOOMSBURY
CHILDREN'S
BOOKS

'I've got this problem,'
said Little Monster.

'I'm sorry to hear that,'
said Father Monster.

'What's the problem?'

'Well,' said Little Monster, 'maybe one day I'll want to be an explorer.'

'Maybe you will,' said Father Monster. 'Is that a problem?'

'Yes, it is,' said Little Monster.

'You see, if I'm an explorer, I'll have to leave you both behind.'

'Well,' said Father Monster,

'maybe we could come with you.'

'No, perhaps not,'
said Father Monster.

'So where will you
explore?'

'Don't be silly,'
said Little Monster.

'Explorers
don't take
their mummies
and daddies.'

'Well,
I'd really really like
to go to the Moon.
Did you know that on the
Moon you can jump as high
as a house because there's
no air to weigh you down?'

'I said
as high
as a house,'

said Little Monster.

'I didn't say
as high as
Space.'

'Don't forget to look up at the sky.
You might see Mummy and me
waving from Earth,'

said Father Monster.

'You'd be much too far away to see,' said Little Monster.
'But I would send you a bit of moonrock
for a present.'

'Thank you very much,'

said Father Monster.

'We'd put it on the mantelpiece

next to the clock.'

'And when I've finished on the Moon,' said Little Monster,

'I'll go on to Mars.'

'Watch out for all those Martians,'

said Father Monster.

'There aren't any Martians,'

said Little Monster.

'Are you quite sure about that?'

said Father Monster.

'Of course I am,'

said Little Monster.

'Well, I am nearly.'

'Then next maybe I'll go on to Jupiter.

Did you know Jupiter has sixteen moons?'

'That's
a bit greedy
of Jupiter,'
said
Father Monster,

'when we
only have
one.'

'And it has
a big red spot,'
said Little Monster,
'and nobody knows
what's in it.'

'Maybe
a big RED dragon,'
said Father Monster,
'waiting
to eat you up.'

'Well
I would
probably
avoid him,'
said Little Monster.

'And then I'll go on to Saturn
and see the rings.'

'Careful you don't slide off,'

said Father Monster.

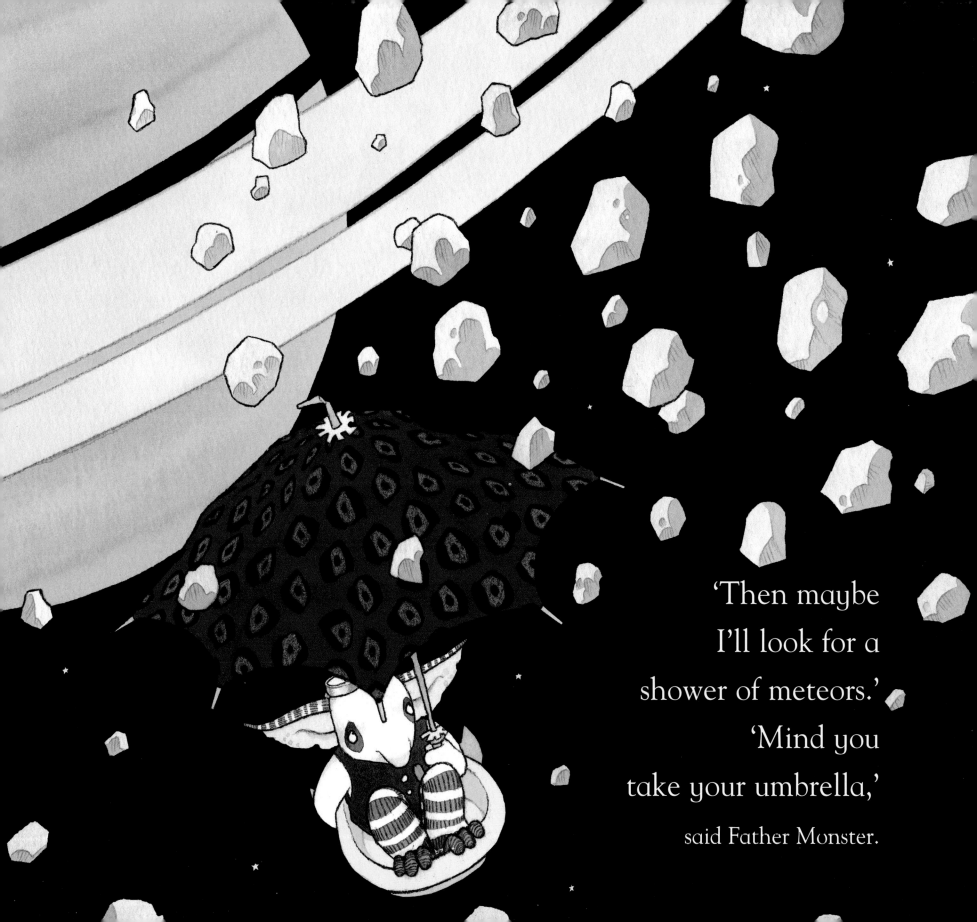

'Then maybe
I'll look for a
shower of meteors.'
'Mind you
take your umbrella,'
said Father Monster.

'And if I see a comet with a long long shining tail, I'll jump on it

and ride

all the way
out into space,

beyond
the planets,

until
I get to the

stars.'

'That's a very long way to go,' said Father Monster.
'But I would have to go a very long way, wouldn't I,
to get to the stars?'

'And then,
I shall look for a star that
nobody has ever found before,'

Little Monster said.

'And if I like it
maybe I'll stay there a bit.'

'Won't you be lonely there?'

said Father Monster.

'Yes, but you have to be lonely
to do some things,' said Little Monster.

'And will you come back to us one day?'

'Oh yes, maybe one day I'll come back,'

said Little Monster.

Acclaim for *Maybe One Day*

'An original and unforgettable little monster' *Sunday Times*

'In both text and illustration the juxtaposition of the security of home and the thrill of the interplanetary unknown provides opportunities, well taken, for a humorously original book' *Irish Times*

'In *Maybe One Day* Frances Thomas lets her loveable monster express every child's hopes and fears for the future … Ross Collins' friendly and eccentric illustrations make us feel almost at home in this monstrous yet familiar world' *Junior Education*

Enjoy more great picture books from Bloomsbury …

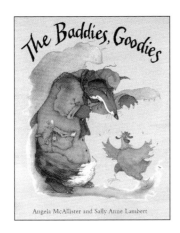

The Baddies' Goodies
Angela McAllister &
Sally Anne Lambert

Busy Night
Ross Collins

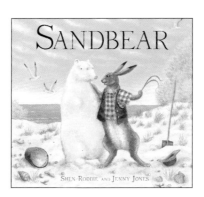

Sandbear
Shen Roddie & Jenny Jones

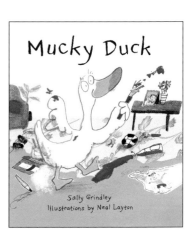

Mucky Duck
Sally Grindley & Neal Layton